OVERSHADOWED

by

CLYDE COLEMAN

First published by AuthorHouse 04/23/04

ISBN: 1-4140-5690-7 (e-book)
ISBN:1-4184-3168-0 (Paperback)

Library of Congress Control Number: 2004090411

This book is printed on acid free paper.

Printed in the United States of America
Bloomington, IN

I dedicate this book to my beautiful and faithful wife Reba. Who lived through this trying time of my life and experienced much of my tormenting thoughts and seemingly foolish actions with out saying a word against me. And to my four older children, Gale, Gary, Greg, and Marsha who were to young to understand why Daddy sat up all night with his big dog and insisted they all sleep together in the big bed. And to my two younger sons, Clyde Jr. and David who reaped many of the rewards of days long past.

iv

Table of Contents

Endorsements

Clyde Coleman is a person of integrity whose character is an inspiration to those who know him. His years of experience, both in life and in faith, have afforded him a wisdom from which much can be gleaned. I believe his writings will be entertaining as well as thought provoking, and have a positive impact upon the reader.

Pastor Stan Sizemore
Faith Christian Center
Cairo, Ga.
(229) 377-8840

I have personally known Clyde Coleman for many years. His life, work and family all give testimony to his love and dedication to the Lord. This short story as seen through the eyes of the main character, Buck Crane, is a vibrant and stirring account of Clyde's personal salvation experience. OVERSHADOWED is a true rendition of the triumph of good over evil and exemplifies the grace of God available to all that seek their destiny in Him.

Robert M. Kirby, Chief, Florida Highway Patrol (Retired) Founder Above the Clouds Ministries, Tallahassee, Fla. www.atcm.us

Introduction

This story is true. Names have been changed. A fictional character, Ol' Massey has been added. Junior's Sea Food restaurant is actually on the dry land not over the water as the story tells. But the "Hell on Earth" the writer experienced was very real. The glorious salvation the writer experienced was equally real and remains so to this day.

Prologue

A penetrating, unearthly murkiness seemed to hang over the house like a great thundercloud. As I sat in the big, deep chair between my bed and the window with rifle ready, watching my wife and children sleep, I felt the cold slime of evil creep across the floor toward us like a damp fog. Exhaustion pulled at every muscle in my body, yet I could not surrender to sleep. If I did—

It was midnight. I had heard it said that evil loves darkness. But this thing had begun stalking me in broad daylight. It had been five days earlier at high noon.

The sun had been straight overhead. I was atop a bulldozer trying to create a firebreak when a curious shape caught my attention. I strained to see through the billowing smoke.

It was—could it be? Yes. The form of a woman, her body covered in blood and ashes, lay in a grotesque heap. Though badly burned, the multiple stab wounds in her back were evident.

From that moment, the shroud of death that covered her seemed to surround me as well, ensnaring me in its folds.

Chapter 1

I was tough. A formidable and demanding father raised me that way. "If a job is once begun, never leave it 'til it's done. Do your work great or small, do it well or not at all." My father had firmly planted that little rhyme in me early in life, and it never left my mind.

Known to both employees and family as Boss Red, my father was a hard-working road contractor. From the office of the War Department in Washington to the ditches where common laborers wielded shovels for him, he was admired, respected, even feared. Boss Red had created a thriving construction company building highways and runways from north Alabama and Georgia throughout Florida and even down into Brazil during W. W. II. And he fully expected his offspring to take his place one of these days.

I also had my nicknames. The state governor referred to me as "one of the RFD boys" because of my laid-back country way of talking. A friend and hunting companion, a United States congressman, fondly dubbed me Cracker. But most folks, the ones that knew me best, called me Hard Rock. As construction supervisor, I had earned that title by relentless tenacity. I had the reputation of staying with a project until it was done and done right. The men in my crews probably felt the handle suited me because of my tough exterior bearing, and some probably thought it was because I was just plain stubborn.

That Monday afternoon when I returned to the construction site after lunch, a thick, white smoke rolled across Highway 98 from a forest fire burning uncontrollably toward Eglin Air Force Resevation.

Eglin would not appreciate people burning her property, I thought. In fact, Eglin did not like people to even be on her land without good reason and proper permits. I was responsible for what happened on this project. So I could think of only one thing to do—contain that fire and put it out before it jumped the highway. But that would not be easy. The blaze was raging, and I was alone.

Standing on the shoulder of the road just outside the present range of the fire was an old, tired-looking, caterpillar bulldozer that seemed anchored to the spot by an old hydraulic blade. The machine was idling, yet there was no operator in sight. Maybe he had gone to lunch with one of the grading crews. Then another possibility flashed through my mind. Had he in some way been caught by the blaze?

That thought drove me to quick action almost

without conscious decision. I mounted the bulldozer, knuckled in the master clutch and started cutting a firebreak on the leeward side of the flames.

For a full hour I worked to partially contain the blaze. Then I circled the still raging flames a second time, cutting a more definitive firebreak. Without stopping to summon help, and knowing the smoke would get somebody's attention soon, I began putting out numerous small fires hoping I could accomplish this task before the forest rangers arrived and started asking questions for which I had no answers. Since it had happened alongside my project, I reasoned that they might expect me to know what or who had started the conflagration.

Preoccupied with that notion, something caught my attention that didn't seem to belong in the bleak landscape left by the flames. A gaseous envelope covered the area, yet through the dense smoke I saw it. No, it couldn't be a body, I reasoned. But there it was, lying on the ground just in front of the left crawler track.

With a reflex that bypassed the thought process, I grabbed the right steering lever and stomped the right turning brake. The big tractor, slack tracks and all, instantly spun to the right spraying ashes into the air and partially covering what had been a white dress with a body in it just inches from the left crawler. I leaned over the side of the old bulldozer and stared in disbelief at the young woman.

It was apparent to me that she had tried desperately but unsuccessfully to outrun her attacker. Like a knife through my midsection, I felt her terror. No doubt she had cried out for help, and no one was there to hear her. No one except her murderer. Had I not gone to lunch, I might have been able to come to her rescue. I very seldom took off for lunch. Why had I chosen to today of all days?

My mind churned at this unpleasant thought. It lodged in my mind and would not leave. But even more disturbing, I wondered what evil force could drive a human being to take another person's life in such a manner?

Oh, I knew it happened—the taking of a life. I had been in military combat. I had perhaps killed myself in the course of duty. But that was war. That was different.

As I stared at her, unable to disengage my emotions from the scene, I saw her in my mind running for her life. She had scurried a hundred fifty feet into the swampy woods from a little three-trail road leading down to the hidden beach on the Emerald Shores. I envisioned her stumbling, screaming, before her attacker caught her and drove the blade the first time into her back.

Finally, I eased the big tractor forward.

My crew and the forest rangers, drawn by the smoke, met me at the edge of the construction site. I explained what I had found and asked the rangers to radio the High Sheriff of Okaloosa County and give him a report.

Later while the rangers were plowing a better firebreak, the body of a man was discovered. A man who looked like someone I knew, someone very close to me. They found him in a palmetto thicket, his upper body charred by the fire.

These events are true. The man and his wife were murdered on Monday June 28, 1954, in Okaloosa County, Florida, between a construction project and the sound on U.S. Highway 98 between Mary Ester, Florida and the Santa Rosa County Line. The crimes were reported in several newspapers and written up in two detective magazines popular at the time.

But this is not the story of those murders. This is the story of Buck Crane, how he lived five days and nights in the shadow of death and came through it with a new life.

Chapter 2

That week, the days seemed to crawl by. The discovery of the murdered family affected me in a way, at the time, I could not understand. Underneath my hard exterior, I was battling indescribable fear.

At first, I assumed it was fear of the unknown murderer. Though I had no reason to believe he knew who I was, I felt he was stalking me and my family for uncovering his evil deeds. During the day I tried to keep focused. The company expected me to finish the project on schedule. And Boss Red was not a man to be trifled with. So I threw myself into my work with all the mental energy I could muster. Still, at night, I was in torment. I could not sleep, and soon exhaustion started to take its toll.

Clyde Coleman

I felt convinced that the murderer was seeking revenge. But there was more. "It" was out there. Somewhere, roaming around just outside of the windows of my home. Sometimes farther out, sometimes nearer in, but always out there, ready to get me if I let down my guard just a little.

Deep within my soul, the nameless fear began to take a form. I knew the color and shape of the beast. I had seen it as a child. In my dreams, after the old folks had entertained us children with yarns and ghost stories, I had seen it.

At that time, it was just a big red butt-headed bull. I lived in dread of it because I knew its intention to do bodily harm to ol' Tom, our family's range bull. My brothers and I had raised Tom from a motherless calf. We had ridden him until he got too big, then we admired him as he out fought all the other bulls my father brought in to build up our herd of Florida scrubs.

As a boy I had feared the imaginary apparition, but now as an adult, a husband, a father of four youngsters, the specter returned to terrify me. No longer was it what I had perceived as a youngster. Now it was an evil, overpowering force waiting to rob me of my soul. It was coming for me and my family. What could I do to stand against such an enemy?

Chapter 3

At five thirty that unforgettable Monday afternoon the last of the work force headed home. I waited alongside the road for my father and brothers. It was our custom after work to stop by our favorite watering hole for a cold one or two where the events of that day were rehearsed and schedules were tentatively set for the next day. The company had two large construction projects underway in close proximity and it was beneficial to exchange ideas.

As I waited, a strong concern for my family came over me. I suddenly had such a longing to be with my wife and children, just to look at them and know they were safe.

This is curious, I thought. Why did I have such a sudden desire to know the children were safe? Never before had I worried about the kids. Millie, my wife, whom I called Mill most of the time, had always been a good mother, never leaving them alone. She was always present to meet their every need. In fact, several years earlier before she and I had become engaged, God had spoken to my heart in a very unique yet unmistakable way that she would be a good mother to our future children.

Don't get me wrong. I knew next to nothing about God. I can't really explain it. I just knew God had shown me that Millie would be right for my children, and that was good enough for me.

So why did I suddenly doubt their safety?

An ominous feeling hung over me. In the same unexplainable way I had known God spoke to me about Millie, I now sensed spirit beings around me. I felt their evil appearances and smells. I knew their names and their intents, though I seemed powerless against them. I felt their barbs pierce my mind with vague fears and confusion.

I could wait no longer for Boss Red and my brothers, Cal and Bo. I had to get home and see Mill and the children. Twenty minutes later, the house was in sight. For a few moments, I felt better. It was a nice country home situated on the sound with a long dock extending two hundred feet into the bay.

All seemed in order. The South Wind, my Chriscraft cabin cruiser anchored in the harbor, two smaller fishing boats tied to the wharf and the Old Town canoe upside down on two sawhorses nearby all waited for me to enjoy them at my leisure. But tonight, the usual pride in my possessions and the thrill of playing with my toys offered no comfort. I wanted to put my arms around my boys and hold my precious daughter on my lap while I watched my wife finish supper.

A good slug of "Who hit John" will get this bad feeling off me, I thought. So I poured a shot of whiskey and downed it in one gulp. But it had no effect. In spite of the good meal Millie had prepared, my anxiety only increased.

Well, since Millie and I had one of the very few TVs in the entire community, some of my kin would soon be by to watch with us and their company would take my mind off this—whatever it was. That didn't happen either.

Too soon it was bedtime. I dreaded the idea of going to sleep. And I was afraid to let the kids out of my sight. I asked Millie to put the children in our king-sized bed with her. The family would all sleep together tonight.

She studied me for a long moment, wondering what I could be thinking. No doubt she could see the trouble brewing in my eyes. Perhaps she attributed it to the trauma of discovering the murdered woman. Whatever she thought, she complied without comment.

But instead of going to bed myself, I moved a large overstuffed chair from the living room into the bedroom. Millie's brow furrowed as I got the 30/30 Winchester hunting rifle from the gun cabinet and loaded it. Then I did the same with my double barreled L.C. Smith shotgun. I checked the chambers in my 38-caliber Smith and Wesson revolver, slammed it into my shoulder holster and stuck the Randall fighting knife, a replica of the one I had carried in combat throughout the South Pacific Theatre of Operation during World War II, under my belt.

Sensing my call to duty, the Arch Duke of Meadow Brook, better known as Duke, my faithful companion and family watchdog, took his place at my feet.

Thus, armed and ready to protect my family against any assault, I began what would prove to be five nights of hell on earth.

Chapter 4

Outside the bedroom window I noticed the low-hanging leaves of the stately old magnolia tremble as if blown by the wind and yet there was no breeze stirring. I imagined the leaves drawing back, repulsed by some evil presence. All natural things disdained the presence of evil. But this would not bother the thing, I knew.

I closed the drapes.

My dog sat at alert. He sensed it out there. He had an awareness of impending danger to his master. But that would matter little to "it" either. The hairs on my arms and the back of my neck bristled. While the thing could not actually see me through the drawn window curtains, I sensed that it was aware of my every move. Its subordinates were reporting. They had been with me all day, hovering over me. They had come with me into the house and were keeping the thing informed.

There were three—the spirit of lying, of fear, and of sorrow—that had taken up residence with me and were teaming up to cause this great worry for my family to come upon me. Though I was aware of their presence, I did not understand what was happening until much later. I also failed to realize that other awesome forces were there to protect my family and direct the warfare I was destined to wage.

The enemy had drawn plans for this siege over many years. Interventions from the forces of God had made adjustments necessary from time to time, but the prince of darkness had great resolve. He was determined to take me even as he had taken so many others.

Overshadowed

The beast had carried out other campaigns against me. When I was twelve years old my grandfather had taken my mother and me to a little church he had helped to start on the banks of the East River. An old country preacher by the name of Taylor had preached his heart out and extended an invitation for those who wanted to be "saved." Though I was under strong conviction, I refused to heed the preacher's warnings and my mother's prayers. I allowed Satan to deceive me and I set my heart to go my own way.

Knowing that if I died unredeemed my soul would be his forever, he had tried on several occasions to take my life. Many times I was only seconds from death. In combat during the battle for the liberation of the Philippines in W.W. II, God spared me from death over and over again.

Clyde Coleman

Later, in a naphtha-filled asphalt barge at West Bay, a valve had been left open, the handle removed, thus making it impossible to pump asphalt from the other compartment until the valve was closed. I stupidly entered the potentially deadly space without a breathing device in order to secure the valve. Proud and vain, I thought I could do anything I set my mind to. I came close to making a good woman a widow that day. But a force—a guardian angel perhaps—lifted me just far enough through the hatch so I could breathe fresh air.

Again, in Port St. Joe, I was spared. A large section of road was burning with intensity and I ran through the flames to close the main valve on a Woods mixer in order to extinguish the blaze the fire department could not control. Though no one saw the great angel protecting his charge and not allowing even the smell of smoke to be on me, I sensed his presence.

For some reason unknown to me or to the forces of evil, God the Creator, had assigned very special angels to protect me. Thus, the enemy's repeated attempts to take my life had all failed—just as Satan had failed in the Great Rebellion before the beginning of time.

Lucifer, the original ruler of planet Earth, called Eden, that Elohim had created to be his footstool, conceived the idea that he could get the cooperation of other angelic beings of the universe and dethrone Elohim to become the exalted supreme ruler of the universe. Why shouldn't they follow him? Was he not the great worship leader, the most beautiful of all God's creatures whose songs of praise and worship rang throughout the heavens? All creation joined in the beautiful singing and dancing of those chosen to lead in worshiping the great God.

Were even Michael and Gabriel, the two archangels, envious of the honor bestowed upon the most beautiful son of the morning? It was well understood by the "anointed cherub that covereth," as Jehovah called him, that he was set aside for some special mission. Why not seize the opportunity and proclaim himself the supreme ruler of the universe? The beautiful one would raise his throne above Jehovah God and become the lord of all.

Lucifer carried out his plan. He instigated rebellion and persuaded everyone possible to join him. He openly broke relations with God and His government, and led his forces from the appointed place of mobilization on Earth into Heaven to dethrone God.

However, he was met by Michael and the faithful angels, and was defeated and cast "as lightning" back to the Earth.

When, through pride, he fell and fomented rebellion against Elohim, he caused his own earth kingdom subjects and one third of God's angels to rebel with Him. So God completely destroyed Lucifer's kingdom on Earth and cursed the Earth by destroying every bird, animal, fish, city, inhabitant and all vegetation. The Earth was snapped several degrees out of plumb. By means of a great flood it was made empty and barren.

It had been a great and glorious scheme. Unfortunately, things had not worked out as planned. One third of God's creation was cast down and scattered throughout the heavens. The planet cursed, snapped out of alignment and tilted several degrees to one side, all peoples and their cities destroyed, not even a bird could be found. The sun refused to give it light. The earth had become desolate, covered with darkness and water. Judgement, for the first time, had come upon the earth because of the sin of rebellion.

Chapter 5

"Are you still awake?" Tuesday morning, Millie swung her feet to the floor and sat up on the far side of the bed.

"Yeah," I replied. "Didn't sleep a wink." I felt angry with myself for being so foolish. Day was breaking in the east. And as the world around me was waking up, the fears of the night seemed ethereal. "How 'bout some breakfast, Mill?"

"Sure, Hon. Let me wash the sleep out of my eyes first." She yawned and headed for the bathroom, then called over her shoulder, "What would you like?"

"How 'bout some grits and eggs? 'Bout four of 'em. Couple links of sausage and some biscuits?" I replied, putting my guns back into their cabinet where the children could not reach them and placing my Randall knife back in the top dresser drawer.

"Toast alright?" came the garbled sound somewhere between the toothbrush and the mouthwash. "Biscuits take too long."

"OK, I guess. I'll feed Duke and check the boats. Don't wake up the children. Let them sleep a while longer."

I opened the door into the carport on the opposite side of the house from the bedroom. It was as if I stepped out of a storm into world renewed. Daylight from the east was chasing the darkness. A light breeze from across the sound, not strong enough to make waves, made light ripples on the surface of the water. The boats gently tugged at their mooring lines. A mocking bird announced the coming of the day.

Last night was a bad dream fading away as life came back into everything around me. It was good to be alive.

"Buck, what in blazes happened yesterday? Did you really walk that dozer across that boggy swamp?" Boss Red asked as he drove up to where I was inspecting a drainage structure being finished by the concrete crew. "Do you know what it would take to get that tractor out of that bog hole?"

Before answering, I quickly reflected on what now seemed a foolish move on my part. Boss Red had that effect.

In all the years of operating heavy construction equipment, I had never placed a piece of machinery in such a perilous situation. The fire was burning deep into the west side of the boggy swamp. I was on the east. Tall Bay trees and Ti Ti bushes made up the vegetation. The water, only one foot deep, was under-laid with a thick layer of muck capable of burying the bulldozer up to the operator's platform.

I recalled that a brief prayer, something like, "God help me," almost unconsciously had escaped my lips as I pointed the caterpillar westward and began pushing down trees ahead of me. It was a crazy scheme, completely unorthodox, but it had worked. I crawled the old bulldozer from tree to tree forming a mat underneath me on which to work from. It must have been one hundred and fifty feet across.

My heart was pounding like a trip hammer, yet I had no fear. After thinking it over carefully in those few moments, I felt justified, foolish as my actions may have been. A feeling of peace and confidence came to me. "To tell you the truth, Boss, I guess I didn't think much about it. I knew two things. There was a fire burning toward Eglin Reservation and I was alone. So it was up to me to stop it. The swamp was not the challenge, putting out the fire before it jumped the road was about the only thing I was thinking about."

"Well," Dad said in an uncharacteristically gentle tone, "you did a good job, Son." He very seldom called me son. "You did the right thing." Then Boss Red surprised me even more. "I'm proud of what you did."

Those were words seldom spoken by my father. He was not one to pass out compliments indiscriminately.

"Dad," I interrupted and surprised both of us—I always called him Boss—"what would it be like to be caught in that wild fire? What was it like at West Bay?"

Clyde Coleman

I knew the story well. The company, our family business, had been under contract with the state of Florida in 1934 to build a sand and asphalt-based highway from West Bay to the Gulf of Mexico. There were very few hotels and no motels between Panama City and Pensacola in the mid-thirties so the crews had lived in tents on the job site.

About midnight one night in the early fall, Billy Joe Williams, a foreman sleeping on the site, was awakened out of a sound sleep by a distant explosion. Instantly, the night sky glowed with the light of a great fire. He quickly woke every man in the tent and they hurried through the deep sand ruts to the barge landing on West Bay about a mile away. The fire could be seen for miles. They realized that one or both of the barges, one of steel and one of wood, that supplied asphalt to the job had blown up and had become a raging inferno.

Boss Red and the pump operator had been tending the barges. Dad had been walking along the deck of the floating steel barge that night. It lay low in the water, loaded with volatile cut-back asphalt. The wood barge, half empty, moored along side.

A spark from somewhere ignited the naphtha and the explosion threw Dad fifty feet into the salt water of the intracoastal-waterway and, as we found out later, killed the pump operator. Everything was burning. Instantly, liquid fire covered every square inch of water for hundreds of feet in every direction.

Boss Red managed to get back onto the steel barge by climbing hand over hand up a burning rope to search for the pump operator. Not finding him, he dove into the flaming waters again and swam underneath the surface toward the beach, coming up for air several times.

When Billy Joe and the workmen arrived at the beach, Boss Red, his leather jacket the only piece of clothing intact, his head and hands burned badly, was wading toward the shore calling on God for mercy.

I was only ten years old when my mother took me to visit him at the Millville Hospital. I would never forget how he looked that afternoon, his face and head covered with a thick black substance. Electric light bulbs surrounding his upper body and legs, supposedly drawing the heat from the burns. His hands were heavily bandaged. I could see the pain in his eyes. I remembered how I wanted to take that pain from him and would have given anything for him to be able to get up from that bed and come home with us.

Almost every church in the Florida panhandle had prayed for Dad that Saturday night. Instead of dying as the doctors had predicted, he began to improve. It took years for him to regain his strength and dexterity, but he did recover and became a better man than ever.

Yes, I knew the story well, but my father had never told me what it was like to be caught in a wild fire and burned nearly to death. Neither did he tell me now.

I could see the pain in his eyes as he remembered the past. For a moment his thoughts were arrested by the minutes in the fire, the weeks in the hospital and the years recovering his strength.

I could readily see that he fully understood what his son had gone through the day before. Fire raging all around. Smoke so thick breathing was difficult. Working by feel and a sense of direction alone. Finding the way out of the haze only to realize the need to go back again.

I never felt closer to Boss Red than at that moment.

Chapter 6

Working on the project Tuesday, some of the crew discussed the findings of the previous day in more detail. I was relieved that the memories did not cause the fears to return. But that was daylight.

Late that afternoon apprehension met me at the entrance to the driveway. It was weird. I had a strong urge to turn around and leave. At that time I could not understand it.

Despite the feeling, I parked in front of the house. All three boys, Gale, Gary and Greg, burst out the front door and ran up welcoming me with the usual tackles and roughhousing.

Millie followed holding Marsha, our daughter, offering more sedate hugs and kisses. All glad to see me. Some wanting to go for a boat ride, some wanting to go crabbing. But Mill wanted us to have supper before it got late.

Secretly I was on my wife's side. Supper sounded good to me. I had not stopped for lunch that day. But I dreaded the coming nightfall. So partly to satisfy the children and partly to stave off the close of day as long as possible, we all boarded the larger of the two fishing boats, cranked the outboard motor and ran down the bay about a mile.

It was peaceful cruising along at half throttle with just enough spray blowing over the bow to make the trip exciting for the children. The sun was submerging itself in the west end of the sound as we returned and tied up to the dock.

Duke ran up trying desperately to wag his short tail to greet us back to land. A dark thought preoccupied me. It was time to go into the house and face another night like last night.

Now what made me think that? I wondered. Why should I not eat supper and then enjoy a much-needed night of sleep? I had no reason to believe this would not be a normal evening with my wife and children. But still the thought persisted.

After supper, Millie busied herself clearing the table and washing dishes. The oldest of the boys quietly read a book and I tried to entertain the younger children with some games. But my mind was not in it. I was thinking again about what might be outside the bedroom window.

Fear kept growing in my mind. Finally, I mustered the courage to take Duke and patrol outside. Armed with my 30-30 Winchester, I should have felt safe enough. I had been through combat in the South Pacific. I knew what it was to face the enemy at close range.

I was not without fear over there. But this was different. I had no tangible enemy to justify the way I felt. I knew there was probably nothing there to hurt me or my family. Yet I couldn't explain away the eerie foreboding. I was out of the house, in the yard. The moon was giving some light. No monster was visible to my sight. Nevertheless the hairs on the back of my neck were standing up.

It was time to go back inside. As I turned my back, I sensed the presence behind me. I stopped. I can't explain how, but I could sense its thoughts.

"What are these weak mortals doing on this planet? Was the Earth not given to our 'most worshipful leader,' the 'king of Tyrus' in the eternity past?"

The creature recalled when Lucifer was given dominance over Eden, the garden of God. It remembered the end of the "Great Rebellion" when it and its fellows had fled from the judgement of God and become outcasts.

They remained rebels and were still at large in the heavenlies when Eloha moved upon the face of the waters and Elohim recreated the Earth.

After light was released on the great flood, the Earth restored to a habitable state, after new land animals, fish, fowls and vegetation were created, then Adam was set up as new ruler. That was not fair. Lucifer was stronger, more beautiful, a greater leader than this puny race called man.

I felt frozen to the spot. Not accepting defeat, it praised its supreme leader that he, with the help of the serpent, had deceived the woman and coerced her into enticing her husband to rebel against God.

The rebellion continues. Victory is certain. Soon Lucifer will ascend into heaven and exalt his throne above the stars of God. He will sit upon the mount of the congregation in the sides of the north.

But now there is work to do. The spirit of anxiety had met the man as he drove slowly down the driveway that afternoon. The orders were to attach to the man and create a despair of life. The efforts were weakened when the family joyfully met him with love and respect. However, when the man returned from the trip down the bay anxiety and fear met him. They will hover throughout the night, giving him no rest. Piercing his mind. Preparing his soul for the time when he will turn his back on God forever.

Was this all my imagination? If it was, why were the hairs on Duke's back standing on end?

No, there would be no sleep tonight.

Chapter 7

Daybreak Wednesday found me in the shower trying to wash off the dreadful feelings of the last several hours. My mind was slow to react because of the impressions that had lingered with me throughout the night. It was as though I was mentally walking through thick mud.

Wake up, ol' boy, I told myself. It's only been two nights. You've gone longer than that without sleep. Get a move on.

I tried to get dressed without awakening my wife. But Millie had coffee on and was cooking bacon by the time I got to the kitchen. I declined her offer of breakfast. There was no way I could eat. "Just fix me a thermos of coffee," I growled. "That'll be enough."

Clyde Coleman

At the construction site, I felt better. I was in my element. This was my turf. I was in charge.

For some reason, I remembered my guardian angel. Could it be the angelic beings were surrounding me now, keeping the powers of darkness at bay so I could accomplish my work during the day?

No, that was preposterous. Where did ideas like that come from? I'm just rough and tough and hard to bluff, I thought. No demon or man can stop me on the job.

"Mornin' Boss," came a hearty greeting from my concrete foreman, Major Grimes, standing knee-deep in mud and water at the end of a flooded concrete structure. "Seems like the ol' mud hen conked out on us last night. But we'll get 'er dried out in a couple hours and still make our pour on time."

Major was a good man. Probably a Christian, I thought. At least he did not allow any cussing in his crew.

"Good morning, Maj. I'm not surprised that old pump gave up the ghost. It lasted a year longer than I thought it would. I'll requisition you a new one. Have it to you by tomorrow. Anything else I can do for you?"

"Yes, siree!" he laughed. "You can pray it don't rain this afternoon. We can't handle any more water." The foreman turned away to help his crew prime the other pump. A centrifugal. "This'll snatch that excess water out of here in a hurry," he called.

It was not unusual for Major to talk about praying. When I thought about it, I realized he seemed to pray about most everything.

I drove slowly through the project, observing

each operation with an expert eye, knowing where each man should be working and where each piece of equipment should be operating. All was moving smoothly.

On my second trip through, I stopped by the "lay-down" crew. Billy, my brother, asphalt boss, assistant superintendent and my right hand man came over to the pickup. "Have a cup of coffee Bill?" I offered. "It'll cool you off."

"You're right, big brother. Just about anything is cooler than hot mix asphalt on a hot July day."

"Billy, it's only June the thirtieth. July don't start 'til tomorrow. That's when it gets hot. And it's only eleven o'clock in the morning." He sipped his hot coffee from a metal cup. "Anyhow, no use looking for shade this early in the day. We've got a few hours ahead of us before you can holler for the calf rope."

Before Billy could respond, a short blast from a siren sounded. Turning, Billy and I saw the High Sheriff's car pulling alongside my pickup. The Sheriff signaled for me to follow him.

Without hesitation, I pointed my forefinger with the thumb cocked at the car, acknowledging the command. Taking the empty metal cup from my brother's hand, I drove to where the sheriff's car had pulled off the road and parked under a large shade tree. I stepped out of my truck and strolled up to the squad car.

The lawman opened the door and extended his right hand for a hearty handshake. When I took his hand, he pulled me halfway into the car.

"Buck, I want you to meet somebody," he said as I unexpectedly came face to face with his passenger. "This is the man that killed Jackson and his wife last Monday." Sheriff Harvell paused a moment to wait for my reaction. "I arrested him a few minutes ago and wanted you to see him before I took him to jail."

I looked deep into the eyes of the handcuffed killer. What I saw gave me a cold chill on that hot day. I found no remorse there. Only a sort of deadness. Darkness.

"Thanks, Sheriff. Lock him up tight," I said. "I appreciate you thinking of me."

After the Sheriff's car and the other law enforcement vehicle were gone, I climbed back behind the steering wheel of my pickup and sat there, motionless. My mind was churning. How could any man take the life of another person and be so unconcerned about it? No regret. No repentance at all. What evil forces lurked in the mind of a man committed to destruction? I wondered.

I drove off the project that afternoon assuming my problems were over. Since the killer had been apprehended, what more did I have to fear? Yet even as I thought that, the same dread that had gripped me the last two nights began to descend. One dark thought seemed to cling to the corners of my consciousness: What evil lurked in the mind of a killer?

As I approached the house, knowing my family was inside, I entertained a new fear. Was there any way that cold-blooded killer could escape from jail and attack my family?

Of course not, I tried to reassure myself. Sheriff Harvell's jail was breakout proof. But why was I so afraid? Why this sense of impending doom? I would guard my family to the death. But what if that was not enough?

Clyde Coleman

Chapter 8

Wednesday night the torment did not let up. I felt the demonic spirits closer that ever to the bedroom window. Again the hairs on my neck bristled. From time to time, Duke, the faithful watchdog sitting at his master's feet, would emit a low-pitched growl from deep within, warning me of present danger.

I know now that nothing of natural substance can come against a spirit being. Neither can a spirit being physically force his way into a natural body without proper invitation. His only tool is deception. And while the dog was not deceived, man's natural mind is easily deceived. A gift from Eve, the mother of all living.

I knew from listening to my grandfather when I was young that in the beginning Lucifer had clothed himself in the body of the serpent because it was the most subtle of all the beasts God had made before he spoke to Eve.

"You shall be as God, knowing good and evil," he told her. With half truths and vague promises, he deceived her.

I was about to discover that the most powerful weapon—possibly the only weapon—the devil, our enemy, has to use against the human race is deception.

During my tour of duty in WWII, I had learned how deception could be a very effective tool in the right hands and used properly.

In 1944, I had turned down a commission in the army at Gordon Military College and again in the coast artillery in order to qualify—I thought—to enter into pilot training in the Army Air Corps.

Turned out they decided the Air Corp had

enough plane drivers, and the Battle of the Bulge changed a lot of people's minds about warfare. Though I had qualified for pilot training in CTD, to my extreme disappointment, I was earmarked and sent back to the previous job I had trained for, the artillery. For the first time in my adult life, I cried.

I arrived at headquarters battery with a chip on my shoulder about the size of Texas. And with good reason. I had turned down a commission twice. I'd flown an airplane for a few hours. I'd worn officer's pinks and liked the feeling of being in command.

My commanding officer, a captain in a heavy artillery battalion, was a large man. He had been a schoolteacher in civilian life, but as an officer in the army, he was in just for the duration. Like the rest of us, he just wanted to do his time and go home. I was assigned to his battery three months before we shipped out for the South Pacific.

We had a mutually repugnant relationship. I saw him as an oversized oaf. He saw me as a young upstart in need of a good lesson. Unfortunately, the situation crippled any chances of me moving up in rank.

It probably cost me more than it did him, but we were both losers. We were both deceived. My foolish pride kept me from doing what I knew I should, and because of it, I paid dearly.

Yes, I knew about deception. But I had not learned what the master of deception could do to me. Not yet.

Chapter 9

By Thursday night, I did not want to go home and face the battle again. Yet I still felt the strong need to protect my family against an evil I could not pin down.

As I drove up to the house, I stomped the brake bringing the pickup to a skidding halt, then slowly drove down the driveway, observing all things that came within the parameter of my vision.

A cold chill pierced my being as the icy fingers of fear gripped my heart. For an instant I was looking inside the house. "No!" The word erupted from my lips. "It can't be! I don't believe it!"

Just then my three sons piled out of the house and ran to meet me as I emerged, shaken, from the truck. Cold sweat stood in beads on my forehead.

"How are my boys?" I asked distractedly. "Where are Mom and Marsha?"

"Daddy, Daddy," Gary whimpered, "Marsha fell down and hurt herself and she had blood on her face." Marsha, near two years old, had been born on Gary's fifth birthday, so he thought and acted as if she belonged to him alone.

"What happened?" I asked, turning to Gale, the oldest. "Oh, she just bumped her head on the kitchen table running after Gary." Just older than Gary, Gale, already seven, had ridden the school bus all the way into Fort Walton Beach last term. He took a more mature approach to life. "It didn't hurt much, just bled a little bit."

When I entered and saw Millie standing at the kitchen door, I could tell she had not had one of her best days. Well, I hadn't either. Seemed everything that could go wrong did.

Overshadowed

I still hadn't figured out what made ol' Massey, the state road inspector, lost his temper. He seemed to have a cocklebur under his blanket when he got to the job that morning, quarreling and complaining about the asphalt mix not being hot enough. It was well within tolerance, maybe on the low side a little but nothing that could not be corrected. And Billy did correct it. Quickly. But ol' Massey had continued to fret throughout the entire morning.

About noon, two out-of-state cars had a fender bender just ahead of the lay-down crew. That was costly to the company in time and money. It had nothing to do with the work, but since it happened within the construction zone, it delayed the asphalt laying for about an hour. Ten trucks loaded with hot mix parked, plant crew and lay-down crew standing down. The entire paving operation idle while the Highway Patrol investigated the accident and tow trucks removed the wrecked vehicles. At least no one had been hurt. I had seen too many accidents where people were killed or severely injured.

Then late in the afternoon, Boss Red blew his top and chewed me out for something that happened on the Hurlbert Field project. It was not unusual for the Boss to lose his temper and fuss at me for what someone else did wrong. But today was not a good time for it. As always, I held my peace, not arguing with Dad, trying to understand what the real problem was. But it seemed completely senseless. Finally, I turned and walked away. I had never treated my father like that before, and I felt guilty for having done so. But enough was enough. I was just plain tired of being a scapegoat.

No, I had not had a good day. And now my wife had her hackles up. Wasn't this thing ever going to end? I had lived through hell all week. Would I be able to get any sleep tonight? Probably not.

"Where is Marsha," I asked with a slight edge to my voice. "Is she alright?"

"She's in her crib," came the reply, returning my tone of voice. "She cried herself to sleep. Don't wake her up. She will be all right. Just a little bump. No big deal."

"It might be a big deal if she is hurt. How much did she bleed?" I went into the bedroom. I knew I had no right to fuss at my wife. She had done nothing wrong. I just seemed powerless to control my irritation.

As I looked down at Marsha's little round face, she sniffled just a little. Tears had stained her face and the bump over her left eye was slightly discolored. Of course it was no big deal. These things happened all the time. But it should not have happened today.

I did not enjoy supper. I ate quietly, setting the atmosphere for everyone. The meal finished, the boys got ready for bed. Millie went about clearing the table and washing the dishes. No boat ride. No TV. No fun. I was miserable. It was well after sundown and darkness had imposed its will on all the land. With it, an eerie darkness had invaded the house and it was imposing its will on me and my family. Not a normal darkness as we know it, but a darkness that was felt rather than seen. A darkness that infiltrated the well-lit rooms and impregnated the very walls and ceilings of the house, causing a murkiness that seemed to absorb the light.

"I'm going to read a Bible story to the children and put them to bed," Millie said, as she dried her hands after putting up the last of the supper dishes. "Where do you want us to sleep tonight?"

"Every one sleeps in the big bed," I snapped.

"This thing is not over yet! I'm going to walk outside with Duke."

I started toward the door, then stopped. "Mill," I began hesitantly, "sorry for quarreling." Then I tried to justify my actions. "I have had a bad day."

Quite frankly, I expected her to understand me but I had no inclination to try to understand her. "It's OK," she said, but didn't warm very much either.

Being outside the house had a weird effect on me. The moon was casting a ghostly light on the buildings and trees. A thin mist was moving in from the bay. There was something strange about the big magnolia near the bedroom. Its branches seemed to shelter a thicker darkness than the shadow under the pear trees. Probably because the leaves are thicker,

I told myself. Yet as I moved closer, Duke growled and pressed his body against my leg, blocking my forward movement.

"Stop, it Duke," I said. "I don't like the way you're acting."

He whined.

"Let's get back inside."

What a weakling! I thought. But I couldn't shake the ominous feeling that I would soon be history. I could nearly hear the bullish sounds from the thick darkness under the magnolia. I subconsciously knew that plans had been carefully laid against me, and if I was not extremely carefully, it would culminate in a great victory for the enemy very soon. I could not last much longer under this pressure.

Lying spirits continued to try and convince me that I was alone in this struggle. My fevered mind suggested even my wife was against me. She was more interested in the children than her husband. Boss Red had little respect for me. Far from excellence, which was always the goal I struggled for, my work was sub-standard, the inner voice told me.

I didn't know at the time that all week long deceiving spirits had tried to convince my wife, sleeping beside our children, how little her husband really loved her. She had lived with him in marriage for eight years and she had never seen him act like this before. What in the world obsessed him to sit up night after night with all those guns and the dog? He acted as if someone or something was about to attack. Was this a throwback to times he had killed the enemy during the War? Or when he was missing in action for two dreadful weeks? She had heard

Mr. Crane talk about it once but Buck had never talked to her about his combat experiences. She had over-heard some of the war stories the men in the community passed around. But it had always been her opinion that they were mostly tall tales.

As I sat in the big chair that night, I was convinced of the intensity in the darkness under the Magnolia tree. I imagined the figures merging together with nothing but evil on their minds. Would the sun ever rise again?

I wondered about the angelic beings from my past. Were they also assembled around the house? Occasionally I did feel a surge of strength from deep within. It told me I could hold on a little longer. Everything would be alright. But could I? Then the darkness would surge through me again.

Chapter 10

"No! I already said I don't want any breakfast! I just want to get to my work!" I yelled over my shoulder Friday morning on my way out the door, not caring that I left my wife near tears.

Four nights without sleep, my work being questioned by my superiors, I justified myself. I'd had enough. If one more thing went wrong, I would fire the entire outfit and start from scratch.

Actually, I had no intention of doing anything like that. I respected my crews. I loved my work. I enjoyed being one of the rising young stars in the road-building profession. Even the governor was my personal friend. Had he not once visited me while I was eating breakfast in the Duval hotel and fondly called me, "Buck, my RFD buddy?"

Yes, I truly loved my position in the community of road contractors. But what was this feeling of despair that I could not shake? I honestly did not know how much more I could take. Well, it's Friday, I told myself, and I'm mighty glad it is.

Remembering it was payday brought a little lift to my spirit. Everyone enjoyed payday, "when the big bird flew." Things would surely be better today.

The first person I met was Tom Calahan, project engineer for the State Road Department. "Buck, you better check the grade on the double-barrel culvert at station 23. It looks like it's been disturbed," Tom said in his dry, flat voice.

"And a good morning to you too, Tom," I quipped. "I'll get Mac on it right away."

Walter MacPherson, my project engineer, had been with me on several large projects. Mac had been my engineer while I was rebuilding one of the runways at Moody Field. We had gone through some rough times together.

"Don't let him use the wrong benchmark," Tom said. "If you pour that structure to the wrong grade, it belongs to you. The state won't pay for a drainage structure that won't carry water downhill."

"Got it, Tom," was the best I could muster as he drove away before the conversation turned sour. I had never watched over Mac's shoulder. The engineer knew his business. Why was Tom on the prod? It was not like him to be so negative. Probably his wife had burned the toast or something.

"Major, get Mac down to station 23 and have him check the grade at the mouth of that double barrel," I instructed my concrete foreman. "Tom seems to thinks the benchmark might have been disturbed and the grade thrown off."

"Nothing wrong with the grade, Boss. I looked at it this morning about daylight. Tom's just got a hair crossways and can't pull it out." I liked my foreman. He was always one step ahead of any situation.

"Well, send Mac down there anyway. I told Tom I would and I'm sure he'll be waiting for him." Then I added hesitantly, "Hey, Maj, let me ask you something."

"Sure, Boss."

"Aren't you a Christian?"

"You betcha," he replied. "Every day of the week."

I paused a moment. "How could God allow such a thing as happened last Monday?"

Major Grimes knew exactly what I was talking

about. He had been the first of the crew to meet me at the burn where the murdered family was found. In fact it was Major who had called the Sheriff.

"Boss, let me tell you one thing," he drawled with a native West Florida accent. "God had nothing to do with them killin's. That was straight out 'a the pit 'a Hell."

I was surprised at what Major said, but even more surprised with the authority with which he said it. "What do you mean, Major?"

"I mean—" then paused for a deep breath. I could see on his face that he knew he was treading on thin ice. No one had ever successfully witnessed to Boss Buck. He told me later he had prayed for this opportunity and he was going to make the most of it. "Boss, God does not go around killing people. He loves every man ever born." Major paused, then continued, as if inspired. "Why, He sent His son,

Jesus Christ, to save us from what happened out here last Monday." He paused longer this time. "No sir, that was ol' Ned himself."

Then he really began preaching. "And if the devil had his way he would take your life, and mine too," he said, jabbing the air for emphasis. "Why, he would drive you crazy if he could and make you take your own life."

I had great respect for my foreman and his entire concrete crew. I had suspected them all of being Christians. But right at that moment, I was not ready for a sermon. Anyway, that message was hitting too close to home. I held up my hand to signal I'd heard enough. "Major, you go get Mac started. I've got to check on the payroll."

What was this uncomfortable feeling? I nervously jumped in my pickup, dropped it in gear and drove off.

I didn't understand then that the Holy Spirit had begun to open my heart, nor did I know that the demonic spirits were hanging around looking for openings as well so they could renew the attack. But I surely knew I'd been witnessed to, and I knew there was more to come. Somehow I sensed that soon I would have to make a choice—between life and death.

The two-way radio in the dashboard of the pickup came alive. "Got time for lunch, big brother?" Billy's voice startled me as it boomed out of the speaker.

"Has a pig got a squeal?" I fumbled to turn down the volume.

I visualized my brother's lanky frame dressed in sun tans, trouser legs rolled up three turns above the ankles over high topped leather boots wearing his cowboy hat probably tilted back on his head. A top rate construction man, Billy Crane had worked with some of the top contractors in Florida and Mississippi before coming back home to work with the family's construction company.

"I'm going to take that as a 10-4. Let's meet at Junior's for some mullet and cheese grits."

"That's affirmative, Boseefus. See you in about thirty minutes."

It would be good to put the project in the background for a few minutes and relax with my kid brother. Billy seldom brought bad news. He had a way of solving problems as they came up.

As my assistant superintendent, he was in charge of paving. He'd been my right-hand man on the large contract at Moody Field. We worked well together. Each knowing the way the other thinks, so we needed very little conversation between us to get things accomplished.

"Mac, did you check that benchmark like Tom wanted?" I asked my engineer before I headed out.

"Sure did," Mac replied. We faced each other through the open windows of our pickups. "She's A-OK."

He dropped his truck into gear, then added as an afterthought, "Boss, did you hear what happened to ol' Massey awhile ago?"

"No. Haven't seen him or heard from him all day. What happened?"

"They rushed him to the hospital about an hour ago," Mac explained. "Think he had a heat attack. It don't look very good for him."

I felt my brow furrow. "That's too bad. Let me know if you hear anything."

My tires shot gravel as I headed out for

Junior's seafood restaurant.

So that was ol' Massey's problem. I felt sorry for the old man.

As the restaurant built out over the bay came into view, Billy was just parking his pickup.

"Did you hear about Mr. Massey," I asked, slamming the pickup door.

"Yeah. Happened right beside the asphalt spreader," Billy said. "He was checking the temperature in the hopper with that long-handled thermometer he always carries when he passed out. Geech was looking at him, and when he saw Mr. Massey stumble, he tried to catch him. Scared ol' Geech. Thought he was dead. But the EMS revived him and he was breathing last I heard."

The two of us found an empty table facing the bay. "You doing all right, Boss?" Billy asked, easing his long legs under the table.

I looked him straight in the eye. He was talking to his big brother, not his boss. "Been a rough week, Bo." I knew my brother had to sense that something was very wrong in my life. "To tell you the truth, I don't understand what's happening. I haven't slept a wink since last Sunday."

Before Billy could respond, Junior—owner, manager, headwaiter and friend—came over. Another time he might have pulled up a chair and sat down, but today he stood, awkwardly. "Sorry to bring you bad news, Buck. Mac's on the phone. Says it's urgent."

"Excuse me, Bill," I said, wearily rising. "Order for me, will you?" I asked and headed toward the phone.

"Boss? Mac. It's not good." Mac's voice trembled slightly. "Mr. Massey never recovered. He died in the ambulance before they got to the hospital.

There was nothing they could do to help him."

I could hardly believe what I was hearing. Ol' Massey had been a state road inspector on many of my projects. Seconds passed in stunned silence. Finally, I managed to find words. "He was a good man, Mac," I mumbled into the phone. "Tough but fair. I learned to build better roads under his inspection. Mr. Massey expected quality. I gave him quality. He was satisfied."

It was an honest eulogy. But my brain was reeling. Three deaths in one week. I don't know how long I stood there in shock. Where was God?

Again, without understanding why, I had an overwhelming desire to be with my wife and children. It seemed God didn't care about anybody. An unnatural sort of despair was coursing through me and I was gradually losing hope.

Finally, I somehow dragged back to the table.

"Billy, that was Mac," I said. "Mr. Massey just died. He never recovered." I let my body droop into the chair. "Jun, give me a cup of coffee to go, will ya? Doctor it up just a little if you don't mind."

Junior knew what I was talking about. He did not sell hard stuff but he always had some around in case of emergencies.

I picked up my hat. "I'm going to skip lunch," I told my brother. "Let's get together later." Before he could object, I was already headed for the exit.

Back at the field office, I picked up the payroll then drove slowly through the entire project several times just to keep busy. All the work was going smoothly. Yet there was a subdued atmosphere everywhere, something hanging overhead like a dark cloud.

Though I couldn't put my finger on it at the

time, it was as if a spiritual darkness pressed over me, smothering me, weighing me down. I sensed that a crisis point was coming. I could not continue this way much longer. But something within me resisted. I would not be pushed into despair. Fight. Keep going. Find the light. Yes. That was it. I had to find the light.

Chapter 11

It was time to "call the dogs and head for the house." That was a common expression in the industry at the end of the day.

The paycheck in my pocket did not bring me much comfort. I could stop by Joe's Liquors, I thought. No, if I wanted something to drink, there was plenty at home. And anyway, I hadn't wanted a drink all that week. It was not what I was looking for. I felt some unidentifiable longing. Nothing satisfied it anymore. Not the work I loved, not my boats or home on the bay, not even my wife and children. I was certain a shot or two wouldn't help.

After going to the bank and making the proper deposits, I drove slowly through the construction site once more and rehearsed the events of the week—

something I did at the close of each workweek. I reflected on the work that had been completed and rehearsed the plan for coming week.

The production schedule was etched in my mind. Over the years, my father had taught me to rehearse what I had accomplished and to know what I was going to do next. So having formulated a rough plan for the coming week, I could comfortably leave the cares of the project behind instead of carrying them home and worrying over them all weekend.

When I reached the west end of the project, I stopped at the burn site. A light breeze blew across the sound carrying a faint fragrance of salt water with it. All was quiet. At that moment, an unexpected sense of peace enveloped me. I felt emotionally at rest. An assurance that everything would be all right settled over me and salved my tired, haunted spirit.

There was mystery here. I knew the scarred land where the fire had raged four days ago would soon turn green with new plant life springing forth from the dead earth. I had seen that happen many times before. The fire had taken life from all the plants in the burned area, yet life would soon be back in abundance.

When I was a child, before Eglin AFB had taken that area from the Department of Agriculture and evicted the entire population, my folks would burn large areas of the forest every year. That would cause the grass to come back richer and greener to enhance the grazing range for our cattle.

Where did the plants that sprung up and covered the blackened ground come from? They must come from God, I reasoned in a moment of revelation. And if God could give new life to the earth, then Grandpa might have been right when he had told us many years before that God could give us eternal life.

I shook my head as if to clear my thoughts. Where did that come from? I asked myself. Later when I remembered that day, I realized the Holy Spirit had been beside me, drawing me. But at the time I could not see the beautiful angelic beings hovering around the pick up.

I was not accustomed to thinking of God at moments like that, but for some reason unknown to me at the time, I felt suddenly compelled to pray. I bowed my head. "God, have it your way," I said softly.

Chapter 12

As soon as I left the sight and turned the truck toward home, the confusion returned. Driving west on US 98 along the snow-white beaches of the Santa Rosa Sound late Friday afternoon, my mind was being pulled by two opposing forces. There was a great calm like a lake hidden deep in a quiet wooded glen protected by high rugged mountains. And there was urgent anger rising like the beginnings of a storm surging, crashing upon the beach, warning of impending danger.

The dark cloud once again filled the cab. Troubled thoughts buffeted me. If there is a God of this universe, he has long since deserted you, my friend. He no longer cares for you or your family. You are now free to be your own man.

I did not like that inference, yet I could not shake it. Thoughts of foreboding began to strike like lightening in my brain. Your time is up. Tonight is the night. You can't protect your wife and children. You can't even protect yourself.

A shaft of cold fear shot through my very soul. My hands began to sweat. I trembled uncontrollably.

Turning into my driveway, I dreaded being at home. As soon as I opened the cab door, Duke unceremoniously flopped his huge front paws onto my lap and barked loudly in my face trying to get my undivided attention. The children bolted toward the truck yelling joyfully. "Daddy, Daddy, you're home. Glad to see you."

Gregory, the youngest, ran up with his arms lifted and said, "Daddy, ride me horse'y back."

My wife hugged me and kissed me on my cheek. "I have a good supper ready. Get washed up and let's eat."

Their overwhelming welcome was a sweet relief. I felt stronger. But thoughts of what lay ahead once the sun went down still taunted me from the shadows.

"That was the best shrimp casserole I ever ate." My wife glowed at the compliment. It felt good to enjoy a tasty supper with such an ever-loving family. "I stopped by the bank and made the deposits. You going to town to shop in the morning?"

"I'm planning on it. The boys need haircuts. What are you going to do?"

"I don't know. Might take the South Wind down the bay." I hesitated, then said, "I'm not sure about anything right now."

"Honey—" Millie reached across the table and grasped my hand firmly. "—tell me, what's wrong? You've been acting so strange this entire week. It's not like you to be this way."

"What do you mean?" Before I thought what I was doing, I spoke more sharply than I should. "What's not like me?"

"Honey—" She spoke slowly and soothingly, still holding my hand. "—I've never seen you afraid before." She smiled with admiration. "I mean, I didn't know you even knew what fear was. You've always been like a rock."

Her sweetness disarmed my defenses a little. I sighed deeply. "You have no idea what I've been through this week. Seems like all hell has broken loose. I just don't know what I'm going to do." I tried to pull my hand away and get up from the table.

Millie tightened her grip and looked into my eyes with a strength of her own. "Honey, you can always pray."

"Pray?" I sneered, not caring how my tone cut her. "Pray'n 's for mothers and children."

The screen door slammed behind me.

Chapter 13

There was a deathly quiet in the bedroom. Mother and children slept peacefully in the big bed.

I did not see the warriors with swords drawn, facing the evil, swirling horde. I did not know of their orders not to interfere with my adversaries. It was my battle to win or lose.

Now I know that they were there to protect, at all costs, the godly mother and her children. Alertly, the shining angels waited, ready to defend but understanding that victory was assured in protecting the family because of "the blood of the Lamb and the word of their testimony."

Clyde Coleman

It was midnight. In the big, over-stuffed chair beside the king sized bed where my family slept, I was aware only in a very general sense of the spirit world in which I was entangled.

I waited.

Duke sat on his haunches nervously peering toward the window. My rifle, fully loaded, rested on my lap along with the double-barreled L.C. Smith shotgun. The Randall fighting knife was tucked into my belt and the Smith and Wesson 38 cradled in my shoulder holster.

Was I losing my mind or were there shadows merging before me? The very air seemed to be thickening. I had difficulty breathing.

I could not see the loathsome creatures throwing darts of cold fear into my heart and despair into my mind. I could not hear them yelling frightening things into my ears. But deep within me I knew they were there. My grip on the rifle tightened. Yet I was beginning to understand that my enemy was not mortal. How could I protect my soul from the invisible yet deadly foe?

At that moment, a low-pitched growl rumbled from deep in Duke's throat. As he rose cautiously, it became a vicious snarl. Across the room, through the closed door facing me the head and neck of a monster slowly emerged. It was the beast I had dreamed of so many years before.

First, it glared my way, then it stepped slowly into the bedroom.

It was a huge beast, much bigger than ol' Tom had been. The thing must have weighed at least twenty two hundred pounds. Its hide was deep red, its eyes like flames burning into my soul. A nauseating odor accompanied it.

Terrified, I could not move. My firearms were forgotten. My faithful watchdog whimpered, cowering between my feet.

Once totally inside the room, it turned and sauntered toward the far side of the bed with a wicked delight.

What was I to do? I realized I was screaming. Yet no sound came. My mouth was thrown open as wide as my jaws would spread, and spasms wrenched my body in scream after scream that tore from the core of my being, yet I was utterly mute.

Chapter 14

Miles away, Spanish moss hanging from the limbs of the giant oak tree swayed gently in the late night breeze. All was quiet at an old frame house along State Road 87 north of the bay.

Woodrow Harold, my mother's youngest brother, sat up abruptly. He was awash with perspiration. What had awakened him? Something must have disturbed the hens in the chicken coop. A fox perhaps, or a possum?

Well old Tige would handle any varmint that might stray by. Tige, short for Tiger, an old Brindle cur hog dog, had helped catch many wild hogs in the East River swamp. Woodrow had raised Tige from a pup along with his own children. He was practically a member of the family.

I'll just get a glass of water and go back to sleep, Woodrow thought.

When he returned from the kitchen and sat back on the side of the bed, a disturbing thought came to him. He had not visited his nephew all week. Feeling guilty for his negligence, he laid his head on the pillow and closed his eyes.

There it was again. Now he knew what it was. A very strong urge to pray for his nephew, Buck Crane.

Unable to put the thought aside, he got up again, pulled on his pants and walked outside. Wondering momentarily why his wife had not awakened, he went to his knees under the big oak and began to intercede for his nephew.

Woodrow sensed a presence beside him. Under the moonlight, as he lifted his voice in prayer, he was aware of a messenger, tall and slender, dressed in a brilliant blue tunic and trousers wearing golden sandals, singing a beautiful song of praise and worship to the Lord in Heaven.

Day was breaking in the east before the duo completed their task.

When Gladys awoke and found Woodrow missing, she pushed the sagging screen door open.

It had been worn out for a year. She remembered when it was new, like the house was then. Woodrow had been in the war at the time. While he was fighting in the frozen mud of the Italian winter, she was building a house for them in the cold wind of the Florida panhandle.

It was a simple frame house. A fireplace for heat. No porches. Steps led from the front yard into the living room and from the back into the kitchen.

There was no bathroom, just a path to a patch of trees behind the hog pen.

One day she was going to build another house. Maybe brick with electric heat and indoor plumbing. But that would come in time.

"Is everything alright?" she called sleepily to the figure under the oak.

"Is now," came the weary reply.

Woodrow was worn out. Never had he prayed so hard for so long. "I have to visit Buck this afternoon and invite him to church tomorrow," he told his surprised wife at breakfast. How many times had he made that invitation? Too many to count.

"Well," he said as if to himself, "one more won't hurt, and maybe it will do some good."

Chapter 15

The brute beast's eyes blazed at the far side of the bed where the children were sleeping. It lumbered past me and nuzzled the youngest. The baby girl continued to sleep. Then it took the small form into its mouth, and with a menacing snort, began to devour the little body.

What is happening, my brain screamed, my vocal cords still frozen with fear. My gaze glued to the horrible sight before my very eyes, I tried to move. My arms would not respond. I struggled wildly, but could not lift a hand of objection.

This cannot be real, I thought. I must be dreaming. But I knew I was not.

The creature continued to feed on the children, consuming them one by one in unhurried pleasure. Its eyes shifted occasionally to me in curious interest.

My God, where are you? my mind screamed. But try as I might, I could not utter a sound. If I could only speak, if I could but utter a small prayer I might drive the beast away.

I tried desperately to speak the name of Jesus. Over and over I tried. Jesus. Jesus. Jesus.

Unable to make a sound and my body was frozen in place, all of my physical armaments lying uselessly in my lap, my tormented spirit accused God for my helplessness. Where was God when I needed him?

In a matter of an instant, my impotent mind vividly rehearsed the past five days, every moment of every hour.

Then it raced backward in time to one night very long ago. Grandpa was reading the Bible. We grandchildren were sitting in a circle in front of the warm fire listening intently to every word. "For God so loved the world He gave His only begotten Son that whosoever believeth in Him should not perish…"

"What does that mean, Grandpa?" asked two of us simultaneously.

Shifting in the old cowhide bottom chair so the kerosene lamp could give him better light on the pages of the much-used old Bible, Grandpa said, "Well, children, that means God loved us so much He let His Son Jesus be crucified on the cross at Calvary to pay for our sins."

"What does crucified mean, Grandpa?" one of the smaller children asked.

"It's the way they killed him, silly," the oldest chirped, showing his knowledge of adult things.

Then my mind leaped to the night at a little country church with sawdust on the floor when I was twelve where I heard my mother cry out for God to save her son Buck. Next I recalled the day when old Brother Taylor, the country preacher, talked to me about getting right with God before I shipped out for overseas combat duty.

I relived the many times on battlefields when I prayed for God to keep me safe and bring me home. God had answered those prayers. I came through the war without a single wound. Why then was God allowing this horrible thing to happen to me? God, you have to do something! my heart cried.

The spirit of devastation mercilessly whipped me with chains of darkness. It seemed I could hold out no longer. Every blow drove unequalled pain and fear into my soul. Blow after cruel blow rained down on my tortured mind, emotions and conscience.

This is the end, I heard inside me. But it was not the end. There was another small voice in my heart, one planted there long before by a loving grandfather and a praying mother.

God, where are you?

He is busy at this moment. A new, melodious voice rose within me. May I help you?

Where are my children? my mind asked. What has become of my wife?

They have gone on before you. The voice paused while I took in the implication. They are waiting for you. Would you like to join them?

There was an almost intoxicating charm in the voice—a female voice. An alluring that stirred some sensual passion in my soul.

Can I really be with them? I asked.

Yes, she purred. You have the power.

How? What must I do? How can I go to them?

I must be crazy, I thought. Yet I seemed

powerless to resist the voice. I wanted to be with wife and children. Still, something within me resisted. I wanted to live. For things to be back to normal.

How can I go to where they are? The thought repeated itself.

You have the power near your heart, came the hypnotic voice.

Suddenly, I could move. My right hand reached for the 38 caliber Smith and Wesson resting in the shoulder holster. Slowly, my hand—as if it had a mind of its own—tightened around the pistol grip and began extracting it from the holster.

My mind was mush. My thoughts moved in slow motion. I desperately desired to be with my family. And yet—

Be strong, have courage, come with me, the voice caressed. Just pull the trigger. It will be over soon.

Then deep within my subconscious, the other voice—the voice of life—faintly cried out. Live!

It came again, somewhat stronger. Live!

Stronger still. Live!

"No!" Words erupted from my throat as if I had broken the surface of deep waters. "I will not to go with you."

As soon as I heard my own voice, I whimpered, "God help me! God save me!"

I looked at the empty bed where the family had been sleeping. "God help me," I whispered through tears. "God save me."

Chapter 16

"Honey, is everything alright?"

Through a haze that had enveloped my being, I heard the drowsy voice from the direction of the bed.

I tried to regain some composure, some sense of being. Stark fear continued to possess my mortal being. My body was shaking as if I had strained every muscle against a physical beating. Perspiration soaked my clothing.

Was that Millie's voice? It couldn't be.

I looked hard, straining to see through the early morning light. Was she—

Yes, it was her. I was sure now. Had I been dreaming? No, I had been awake. And I knew I had looked into Hell.

Was everything alright? That voice inside said, yes. Everything was going to be alright.

"It is now," I said, my throat sore. A shaft of light from the eastern sky pierced the room through a crack between the drawn curtains.

"I want to tell you something, sweetheart," Millie said.

I cleared my throat, then answered hoarsely, "What is it?"

"Over a cup of coffee," she said sweetly.

The eggs and pancakes that morning were the best I remembered ever eating. And the smoked sausage was even better. But the coffee really hit the spot.

"I believe this is the best coffee I've ever drunk," I told Millie. "What was it you wanted to tell me?"

Overshadowed

She fidgeted, twisting her napkin into a slender spiral. "Well—"

Everything about me that morning was at a heightened state of awareness, and I knew Millie had something important on her mind. She was trying to muster her courage to open the treasury of her heart and allow her husband to see inside.

I waited. Any other morning, I might have grown impatient with her reticence and rushed over her tender feelings. But that morning I couldn't get enough of her. I gazed at her, losing myself in the sight of her.

At last, she raised her eyes from the napkin and touched mine. I could see she had made her decision. She would trust me—just this once.

"Honey, I want to go to church tomorrow," she blurted, startling both me and herself.

107

Millie had been raised in church. When she was a youngster, going to church with her mother and father had been an every Sunday affair. She had wanted to raise her children in church. Yet for us, life had not been that ordered. We moved from one construction site to another, sometimes several times a year. We had never been in one place long enough to join a church.

"I mean," she began again in a quieter voice, "could you take me and the children to Billory tomorrow?"

Billory Baptist Church had been built after the turn of the century by two of my great-grandfathers and had been named after one of them. The original building on the bay had been abandoned when automobiles gained prominence and water traffic gave way to land travel. A new building had been erected closer to the highway.

Overshadowed

My aunts, uncles and cousins made up part of the congregation. Uncle Woodrow, Grandpa's youngest son, was a deacon and Sunday school superintendent there.

"I don't know," I said hesitantly. I didn't want to trample her feelings, but I just couldn't commit myself to anything just now. Too much was happening. I had not slept in nearly a week. I still wasn't sure what had happened. It seemed as if day after day a tight band had been drawn ever more tightly around my head.

What did I really want to do? A run down the sound in the South Wind to clear my thinking sounded good.

Or maybe a few drinks. But that thought brought no peace to my mind. I had never found comfort in drinking. I didn't believe a man could hide from his problems in alcohol. I enjoyed the taste and the buzz of it but that was all. No, that was not what I needed now.

"Let's talk about it after you and the kids get back from town," I said.

Chapter 17

There was enough chop in the waves to make the South Wind pound a little, throwing salt spray into my face. I revved the Gray Marine engine to three-quarter speed heading directly into the swells.

"This is the life," I said aloud. Nothing like a little physical exertion to make a person feel alive. I felt invigorated, refreshed. After an hour's ride, I turned and headed back up the bay toward home.

The sun shone silver across the waves. The wind at my back made for a smoother passage than when I had headed into the waves. But as the cruiser sliced though the water, the shroud of death seemed to close around me once again. The strength I had felt before began to drain down and out of my body.

I felt like a soldier returning to a combat zone. It reminded me of times in the South Pacific during World War II when we would leave the main camp position and head toward the observation post on the front lines. We would inform the line batteries of targets and give them proper coordinates so the big 240-millimeter howitzers could effectively fire on enemy positions. Though casualties in my squad were rare, there was always the dread of the possibility of not returning to base camp alive.

The strong chain of darkness once again tightened around my mind as I anchored the South Wind. The spirit of despair sapped my will to live. I was being strangled under a monstrous load I could not move. Slowly, I trudged up the beach to the house.

Millie and the children were not home. The house felt dead and ominous.

The midday temperature had climbed to over ninety. A cold beer, I thought. That's what I need. I opened the refrigerator and reached for one.

At that moment, I heard a car coming up the driveway. I grabbed the cold can, shut the fridge and drew back the curtain at the kitchen window. An old blue car was just parking under the overhanging branches of the live oak tree in the side yard. My face brightened into a smile. Uncle Woodrow, one of my favorite people, stepped out and waved toward the window.

"Hey, Buddy Roe," I yelled, coming out the door to meet him. "Haven't seen you in a while. How you been?"

"Just fine, just fine," he smiled. "How are you?"

"Oh, can't complain, I guess," I replied unconvincingly.

113

We headed toward the water's edge. The wind had died down a bit, and a soft breeze drifted across the sound. All was quiet.

He seemed nervous, fidgety. More bad news? I thought. It was obvious something was on his mind more than an afternoon social call. I could imagine that during his time in Italy during the heaviest fighting of the war, Woodrow had looked into the eyes of many a dog-faced soldier desperate for peace and courage with the same intensity with which he now gazed at me.

I had complete trust in the man. I knew I could talk to him about anything. Yet I felt somehow uncomfortable to talk about what I had been through.

After a long pause, I broke the silence. "Haven't slept much since I found that murdered woman."

He shook his head slightly, as if saying he understood. We walked down the sunny beach, waves lapping gently at the white sand.

"In fact, I haven't slept a wink since last Sunday night," I added, then took a long swig from the cold can, enjoying the sharp taste.

Woodrow stopped. The very atmosphere around us seemed charged as my words hung in the air without reply. He dug his toe in the sand. Finally, he took a deep breath. "How about going to church with me tomorrow? We've got a new preacher, Brother Doc Tanner from over near Crestview. Hear he's purty good."

My own silence surprised me. A quick dodge was in order. I couldn't count the times Woodrow had asked me to go to church. I had always found some excuse or other why I couldn't make it. But this time was different. I didn't exactly understand why, but this time I really wanted to go. I wanted to trade in my old life for a new one. I wanted to know God. But could I? Would God accept me?

In that few moments, a monumental battle raged within me. What could I be thinking, one voice said. I had a good life. I was happy with the way things were. Why would I want to go and mess it up by becoming religious?

Another voice objected, If my life is so good, how come I can't sleep at night for fear my wife and children will be attacked? How come I can't shake this unexplained depression? How come I feel like something's missing and I don't know what it is?

Before I even consciously realized I'd made a decision, I heard myself saying, "Be glad to, Buddy Roe. What time does it start?"

As soon as I had said the words, I thought, Now what'd I go and say that for? I took another drink.

What was wrong with that beer? I felt like gagging. What a terrible taste! Had it gone bad in the can in the last five minutes? With the deftness of an old softball pitcher, I underhanded the can, still half full, into the surf.

"Starts at nine thirty," Woodrow said, grinning.

He shaded his eyes with his hand and looked up the beach toward his car. "Well, I'd better be movin' on. I've got to take the family shopping and it'll be late when we get back. See you in the morning then?"

"See you then," I smiled, feeling suddenly lighter.

As Woodrow was turning his car around, Millie pulled in and waved.

"See you at church tomorrow," he called to her.

When he had gone, she got the kids out of the car, then turned to me. "What did he say?"

"He said, 'See you at church tomorrow,'" I grinned. "Is that a problem?"

She stood there, speechless, not realized her mouth hung open.

"Roe asked me," I said in a matter-of-fact way, like reporting the weather, "and I accepted. He thinks we'll enjoy the new preacher."

That afternoon, red clouds gathered around the sun settling into the mouth of the sound emptying into Pensacola Bay. Quiet and peace seemed to settle over the house for the first time in a week.

The kids slept in their own beds. So did I.

Chapter 18

The sun drove darkness from the sky and assumed it's rightful position, arcing above the earth. A mocking bird sang with gusto, announcing the new morning. It was the dawning of Independence Day.

In 1776, the people of the United States of America declared their independence from a foreign monarch, the King of England. We then went to war, a struggle that lasted into 1787. England was somewhat displeased with the results of that war, so in 1812, they again tried to take from Americans their right to life, liberty and pursuit of happiness. They invaded the land and battled until they conceded their defeat in 1814.

This day, July 4th, 1954, was destined to become a real Independence Day for Buck Crane. After battling the forces of evil for five days and nights with no reprieve, I rose that Sunday morning refreshed by a good night's sleep, guarded by two heavenly figures in magnificent apparel and shining armor.

"Get up, children," Millie called merrily. "Time to get dressed for Sunday school."

"Mommy, can I have some money for the offering?" Gale asked. He was old enough to remember going to Sunday school a few times.

When I pulled into Billory Baptist Church that morning, I noticed it had not changed since Millie and I had said our vows to each other there eight years and two months earlier.

On State Road 87, nestled in a grove of live oak trees heavily laden with Spanish moss, the little church was flanked on one side by a concrete block, three-bedroom dwelling where the new pastor resided. On the other side rested a cemetery with gravestones dating back to the 1890's.

I have come to believe that two sentinels sat on the ridge of the roof of Billory Baptist Church that morning ready to confront dark forces that might come to stop me from making the decision of a lifetime.

"We must be early. No one is here yet," I said nervously.

"They will be soon," Millie answered. "Anyway, I like to be on time."

"Well, you're on time today," I said. "The preacher is probably still asleep."

Before long friends, kin and strangers began arriving—some walking, some driving. Many of them came over to the car and greeted Millie and me. They seemed truly happy to see us there. If they were surprised, they didn't show it. They appeared to be genuinely interested in one of their own that had grown up with them, gone away to war, then to college and was finally back in their midst, healthy and wealthy.

Chapter 19

The singing and preaching service lasted only an hour. But to me, it seemed a very long time. The battle within had not subsided. I wanted to be my own man, not tied down to a church or a religion, much less to a God who might have different ideas about how my life should be run. Still, I longed for the peace and security I had seen in my wife, in my uncle Woodrow, in Major Grimes and others. By the time the invitation was given, I had made a decision.

As the congregation sang "Just As I Am," I felt a strong urge to bow at the altar. I turned, then I noticed big Al Brown, a man much larger than myself, standing between me and the aisle. No way could I navigate that narrow space between Al and the back of the next pew. Well, Al would surely move when he saw me coming.

He didn't. His eyes were closed.

Without hesitation, I jabbed my left elbow firmly into Al's big belly so I could pass in front of him.

The wind rushed from Al's throat with such an odd sound that every head turned and every eye saw Big Al fold and crash back into a sitting position on the pew. Then they watched me bolt down the aisle toward the front of the church.

The new pastor waited at the head of the aisle with two unseen watchmen on either side of him. "Is this the end?" one asked.

"One more test," his fellow answered. "All hangs in the balance until he confesses the Lord Jesus with his mouth and believes in his heart that God raised him from the dead. Then he will be saved. For with the heart man believes unto righteousness and with the mouth confession is made unto salvation."

I, Buck Crane, tough construction superintendent, felt very lost and undone, very small and unworthy that morning.

Reaching for pastor Doc Tanner's hand, I thought I would feel some change. I did not. I still carried a heavy weight. I truly was a sinner. There was nothing righteous about me. I was unclean. More than that, I was dirty, filthy, vile. My membership in the lodge could not save me. Being a good man and treating others justly did not qualify me to come into the presence of God.

I found a spot on the front row and sat onto the pew. Nothing had changed. I felt overwhelmed with despair.

Then words Grandpa had spoken to me long ago came to me. "Only the blood of the Lamb can clean a man of his sins."

How could blood make anything clean?

I knew much about blood. Among the country folk where I was raised, butchering animals for food was a regular routine. Then as a combat soldier, I had seen plenty of bloodshed.

Then it dawned on me. Blood was life. Life was in the blood.

So it was Christ's blood, or rather His life, that was offered up for the payment of my sins. I could understand it now. Jesus Christ had poured out His life on the cross and God had raised him from the dead to purchase me from the enemy. From that terrible creature that had tormented me day and night over the past week.

Yes! I would accept the work Jesus Christ had

done on the cross to pay for my salvation. I would accept Him as my Lord.

But, I wondered, would God accept me?

Then I remembered Grandpa again, quoting the well-worn scripture, "For God so loved the world that He gave His only begotten son, that whosoever believed on Him would not perish but would have everlasting life."

I, Buck Crane, lost and undone, sat on the front pew, while the choir to sang "Just As I Am."

"Dear God," I whispered, "I really want to be saved. I believe what Grandpa taught me when I was a boy."

From the depths of my heart, I prayed silently.

"All that I am, all that I have, I give to you."

In that split second, God spoke to my heart.

"All that I am, and all that I have is yours."

Instantly, the Spirit of God came into my heart. My spirit was reborn. I became a new creation. A new son was added to the Kingdom of God.

In that small chapel while many of the congregation prayed, I saw an invisible, brilliant light burn all shadows away. It drove the darkness from every crack and crevice. The colored glass window behind the choir began to glow. The pulpit shone brilliantly. Standing to my right and my left, two tall angelic forms began to radiate golden light overshadowing their charge as they laid their hands on my shoulders and prayed along with me.

Outside the building, the sentinels radiated unearthly beauty. Their brilliance burned away the shadows, both natural and supernatural. The ghastly red beast vanished in a cloud of evaporating smoke.

A figure robed in a beautiful blue tunic danced upon the winds.

My uncle Woodrow wept uncontrollably, giving thanks to God, his Father. In Heaven, the angels rejoiced around God's throne, and Grandpa smiled.

The service ended, and everybody gathered around me at the front of the little country church. Millie interlocked her arms with mine in the exact spot where we had promised ourselves to one another eight years earlier, rejoicing with me as I received the right hand of fellowship.

"It would be good if these mortals could see this as we do," whispered the tall warrior, tears of joy streaming down his face.

"They will," replied his companion. He stretched both hands toward heaven. "In time, they will see all things as they really are."

About the Author

Clyde A. Coleman (www.clydecoleman.com) was born in the Choctawhatchee National Forest May 14, 1924. After serving his country in the South West Pacific during WW II, he once again entered into the family business of Highway construction. On May 5, 1946 he met and married Reba Louise Smith of Hamilton County Fla. Raising his family and building up the family business was paramount to Clyde. He gave himself to the task of building the best roads and airbases in South Georgia and West Florida. It was on one of these projects Clyde experienced a life changing predicament. This is the first time he has tried to explain what happened during that week of HELL.

Printed in the United States
19075LVS00002B/145

9 781418 431686